The Body in the Van

by

John Messingham

All rights reserved

The characters and events portrayed in this book are fictitious. Any similarity to real persons, living or dead, is coincidental and not intended by the author.

No part of this book may be reproduced, stored in a retrieval system, or transmitted in any form or by any means, electronic, mechanical, photocopying, recording, or otherwise, without the express written permission of the author.

Cover design by: John Messingham

This book is dedicated to Karen.

One

"Right then. Let's see what's been going on here, shall we?" Garner said as he pulled up in his car along with DS Brierton.

Brierton replied "The call said that a body had been found in a van parked in the Wilton Road industrial estate. Rachel Howton has been assigned as the Crime Scene Manager and is already at the scene looking into it."

Garner said sarcastically, "well, at least we know we will get a cheery welcome at her crime scene."

As Garner spoke, they both got out of the car and walked towards where a crowd of people had gathered near a taped-off area within a yard outside two large retail units and as they made their way through the crowd of people, they came to a police cordon tape that had been stretched across the entrance to the yard and was manned by two uniformed police officers, keeping the crowd that had gathered under control and out of the yard.

"Morning Sir, Sarge." One of the officers said as he raised the tape to allow Garner and Brierton to pass under it.

Garner replied "Morning," and carried on walking but Brierton stopped and responded to the officer with "Morning. Do you have any details of what has happened?"

The officer let go of the tape so it would be low enough to show the limit of where the public could go and started to talk to Brierton.

"Not really. There was a call first thing that said the van had been here all night but that the owner of the antique shop in the yard had asked his staff and the staff in the builder's merchant next door, but no one knew who it belonged to, so he called us. A patrol car was sent down to check the van out in case it had been stolen and dumped but when the officers opened the back door, they found the body in the back."

"Right, are the traffic guys still here?" Brierton replied.

"Yes, they're over there in the coffee shop part of the antique shop."

"OK, I'll speak to them further. Thanks."

Garner had made his way to the van where Howton was dressed in her usual all-in-one-white suit and was looking around the outside of the van.

"Morning Rachel," Garner said, "How are you getting on? What have you got for us?"

"Well, I'm in better nick than the one in the back of the van. But you'll need to see this." Rachel replied as she made her way to the back of the van signalling to Garner that he should follow her."

Two

Once they had got to the rear of the van, Howton opened one of the doors. Garner moved forward to get a better look inside the van and saw the body of a young man lying in the back.

Howton said, "see how the body is laying? I cannot be sure, but it looks like he was already dead when he was placed in the van."

Garner looked around the van and said, "what makes you say that?"

Howton's voice changed to a more superior toned voice which Garner recognised. It meant he was about to be on the receiving end of some brilliant deductions.

Howton then started her mini-lecture,

"well, I think he was dead before being placed in the van as there is no blood on the inside walls of the van. He does have a large head wound and the blood-stained hammer lying beside him leads me to believe that is the murder weapon, so, whoever did this was not bothered about people knowing what took place."

Garner said, "So, are you thinking this is a planned or random attack?"

Howton looked at Garner and said, "That's kind of where you come in, isn't it? I will find out more once I get the body and the van back to the station for a better look."

"Do we have any idea who it is? Any id?" Garner asked.

"No, I've not found anything yet," replied Howton.

"OK then," Garner said and before he could say anything else Howton said, "I know. As soon as I can." To which Garner smiled and started to walk over to where Brierton was standing, talking to the traffic officers who were the first at the scene.

Brierton turned towards Garner and said, "These guys were the first on the scene. They checked the van details on the system which came back showing it had been stolen in Cleethorpes yesterday, so they tried the doors and that is when they found the body. So they, set up a cordon around it and called in the details."

Garner looked at Brierton and said, "OK, so we may as well head off back to the station and wait for the report from Howton and see if we can find out where the van was stolen from to see if that sheds any light on the events leading up to the killing."

Garner and Brierton made their way back to Garner's car, got in and headed off back to the major crime team's office at Grimsby Police Station. As they drove back to the station Garner said, "Can you give Allan a call and see if he wants a drink from the canteen." To which Brierton replied, "OK," and started to call back to the office.

Three

As they drove back to the station Garner's mobile pinged with the sound of a text message arriving on it. Garner waited until they had pulled up at some traffic lights before picking up his phone and looking at the message.

He said, "I'm in trouble!".

Brierton said, "why's that?"

Garner jokingly said, "It's from Superintendent Catherine Jones, she wants to see me when we get back to the station and that's never good is it."

Brierton laughed and said, "to be fair, the Superintendent is not easily wound up so it might be good news."

Garner laughed back and pulled away

again, as the lights had now changed to green to allow them to continue. Then once they had made their way back to the station car parking area, they made their way into the building and into the canteen where they joined the queue at the counter.

Garner noticed that Superintendent Jones was already there and had just bought a drink and was making her way to a table.

The Superintendent looked back towards the counter and saw that Garner was there. She pointed to a chair at the table. Garner knew that this was the sign that she wanted to speak to him here, so he nodded and followed Brierton along the canteens counter.

As they got their drinks Garner said, "I am going to speak to the Superintendent now so can you get Allan a drink and take it back to him?"

To which Brierton responded with, "Will do."

As they moved along the counter towards the till area Garner took out his wallet and said "You head back, and I'll pay for these.

What have you got there?"

"Two large coffees, I think we will be needing them today."

Garner took some money out of his wallet and passed it to the person sitting at the till, "OK, I'll speak to the Superintendent and then meet you back in the office."

Once Garner had been given his change, he picked up his drink and made his way over to where the station Superintendent was sitting and drinking.

Four

"Hello Ma'am, how are you this morning?" Garner said as he placed his drink on the table and pulled a chair out from under it.

"I'm fine Robert. I just wanted to see how you were getting on."

Superintendent Jones and Garner's careers had crossed paths on many occasions in the past and the Superintendent was one of the very few people who called Garner 'Robert'.

"Fine, we are just starting on the investigation of the youngster found in the van on the Wilton Road Estate, so we don't have anything to go on yet," Garner replied.

The Superintendent then asked, "How is DS Brierton getting on? I heard she had to hit the ground running on the last case." To which Garner replied, "She's fine, I knew of her before she joined the team and I heard many people saying how meticulous she is about detail, so I'd like to think she's a bit of competition on that front."

The Superintendent laughed and said, "that's good. I also want to speak to you about your dealings with Mick Kurzwell during the Diss murder case. The Chief Constable has asked me to investigate why he was brought in during the case."

Garner said, "that's interesting. Although it turned out that he had nothing to do with the murder, we did find a lot of stuff linked to his drug activities in his office and he did try and run off when we arrived, so we decided to bring him in for further questioning."

The Superintendent said, "right, that's what I expected you to say from reading the reports about his arrest. I'll let the Chief Constable know that as far as I am concerned, he was arrested and brought in as per current procedures."

As Garner was about to speak again his

mobile which was on the table started to ring. He picked it up and answered the call. "Hello." He paused while he listened to the voice at the other end and then said, "OK, thanks. I'll be back soon," and ended the call.

He turned his attention back towards the Superintendent and said, "That was DS Brierton, the control room has confirmed that the van with the body in was stolen locally yesterday afternoon, so they are looking at the ANPR data to work out where it has been since being stolen"

Superintendent Jones said, "OK, I'll let you get back to your office." As she spoke, she got up from the table and as she did, she continued, "keep me updated about the case."

Superintendent Jones then walked away and headed out of the canteen leaving Garner to finish drinking his drink, then he also made his way out of the canteen and headed back to the team's office.

Five

In the team's office, Civilian Intelligence officer, Allan Parsons, was sitting at his desk looking through the ANPR data relating to the stolen van that he had been sent by the station's control room.

While he was doing this Brierton was reading through the reports that had been made by the two traffic officers who had been first on the scene. Unfortunately, these reports did not provide any more details than she and Garner had gained while at the scene. The real step forward would hopefully come when they received the first report from Rachel Howton and with a bit of luck would also include the identification of the victim found in the back of the van.

As both Parsons and Brierton worked away on the respective tasks the door of the office opened and in walked Garner who had made his way back to the office after his chat with Superintendent Jones in the canteen.

"How are we getting on? Anything?" He said.

Brierton looked up from her desk and said, "nothing new in the reports from the traffic officers but hopefully Allan will get something from the ANPR data. How did your chat with the Superintendent go?"

Garner said, "fine, it was about Kurzwell. The Chief Constable was asking about why we had brought him in during the Diss murder investigation. I don't know why but I assume if he is interested then there has either been a complaint made, which I doubt, as I don't think Kurzwell would be looking to draw any more attention to himself than he needs to or there is something bigger going on involving him and they don't want any problems with previous dealings with him."

Brierton nodded towards Garner and said, "oh, I did wonder when you said it was about him as we only arrested him because he did a runner from his office when we arrived."

As Brierton finished speaking, Parsons looked up from his desk and said, "I may have found something here."

Both Garner and Brierton made their way over to Parson's desk and stood behind him while he carried on looking at his computer screen.

Six

Once both Garner and Brierton had made their way over to Parson's desk, Parsons said.

"Let's see if this makes sense, "he paused for a moment, and then continued, "There's no sighting of the van for a few hours after it got stolen because there are no ANPR cameras in the area where it was stolen from."

"The first recorded sightings of the van are when it turned onto Grimsby Road then headed along the road and then up Isaacs hill. It is not seen again until about twenty minutes later when it hits the camera at the roundabout where the high street meets Alexandra Road. The thing is that the ANPR camera at the top of Isaacs hill is out of action at the moment so it could have turned off on its way up the hill before reaching the top."

Garner chipped in and said, "right, so we need to get down to the area around Isaacs Hill and the high street and do some door-to-door stuff to see if anyone saw or heard anything during those twenty minutes last night."

"OK, I'll get onto the control room and get them to put a team together and get down there straight away," Brierton said as she walked away from Parson's desk and back to her own, where she sat down and picked up the telephone handset on her desk telephone.

Back at Parson's desk, Garner and Parsons carried on looking through the ANPR data as Parsons made notes about the route the van took on its way to the Wilton Road estate.

In the background, Brierton was talking on her telephone, "Brilliant, ten people will be a great help, thanks, can you arrange to transport them down to that area and I will meet them there as soon as I can." Once she had finished her conversation, she replaced the handset on the base unit on her desk and prepared to leave the office.

Parsons finished following the van's route using the ANPR data and said, "It looks like the van went straight to the estate and the timings between hits suggest they made no more stops along the way." To which Garner replied, "Good work. It's just a shame there is not a single image of the van before it turned onto the Grimsby Road and of course, the quality of the CCTV never gives us a clear enough view of anyone driving any vehicle around here."

Garner was now making his way back to his desk and as he did Brierton said, "Right, that's me off to meet up with the house-to-house team and knock on some doors. I've got ten officers meeting me down there, so I expect it will take some time." She then left the office leaving Parsons and Garner sitting at their desks.

Seven

A dark blue minibus pulled into College Street and parked a short distance into the road. In the back were ten uniformed police officers that had been briefed on the required task and sent on their way.

Knowing their task was important they quickly set about knocking on doors and when they got an answer asked to speak to everyone in the house about events the evening before.

"We are making enquiries about yesterday evening and would like to know if you saw or heard anything unusual," one of the officers asked a young woman who had answered her door. "No, sorry, but I was out until quite late last night." Was her response.

The officers made their way along the

road, knocking and asking the same question repeatedly, making a note of any houses where they received no answer so they could come back later and noting down the responses from people who opened their doors.

Brierton arrived as the officers were getting into full swing at the task and as soon as she had found a parking space she made her way along to where the minibus was parked. The driver had taken the role of house-to-house team leader while waiting for Brierton to arrive and now she had, the driver was able to get out of the van and join the other officers knocking on doors.

Brierton scanned through some of the sheets of paper that had been placed in the front of the minibus which had the results of various discussions with householders on the road but so far had nothing of any real use. It wasn't until a couple of officers spoke to a resident in a house opposite Cross Street that this changed.

"DS Brierton," Brierton realised one of the officers was standing at the passenger door of the minibus wanting her attention.

"I have just spoken to a Mr Owens along the road, and he says he heard some shouting last night and when he looked out, he says he saw a white van driving off quickly towards the high street."

"Right, OK," Brierton replied, "I'll come along and speak to him.

Eight

Brierton got out of the minibus, closed the door behind her, and walked along the road with the officer to a house opposite Cross Street where another officer was standing with a middle-aged man at his front door.

"Hello Sir, I am Detective Sergeant Brierton. I understand you may have some information for us."

"Yes," replied the man. "I was in my front room, and I heard some shouting outside across the road, so I looked out of my window and saw a white van driving off along the road opposite my house and turning left onto the High Street," he continued.

"OK, can you remember anything that was said during the shouting?" Brierton asked.

The man thought for a moment and then said, "not really, the only thing I think I heard was something like, "Mick's had enough of your trouble, but I didn't really hear or even see anyone out here. As I said, by the time I got to the window the van was driving off."

"Right, that's great sir, if you think of anything else, please call us at the station. This officer will give you our contact details."

Brierton looked around to see if any of the buildings in the area had CCTV cameras on them and noticed a very small one that unless you were looking hard you would not see it. It was on the side of a small retail shop at the junction of the two roads where the house-to-house enquiries were being conducted.

As she was crossing the road towards the shop her mobile rang. She looked at her phone and saw it was Garner calling her, so she answered the call and said, "Hello Sir."

Garner said, "Hi, Rachel Howton has sent

us some preliminary results about the Wilton Road victim. Can you head back and meet me in the office."

"OK, I'll head back now," Brierton replied and ended to call.

Brierton was now on the other side of the road so looked back over the road and caught the attention of another uniformed officer standing there and beckoning them to come over the road to her side, she then said, "can you speak to the owner of that shop," pointing to the shop that had the camera attached to it, "and ask them if they have any video footage from last night. If so, can you get it and send it to me please?"

The officer replied, "will do Sergeant,"

Brierton then finished by saying, "I am heading back to the station now so can you all keep knocking on doors? I will read the reports as soon as you all get back to the station as well."

The officer said, "OK, we will be as quick as we can." The officer then made their way towards and into the shop.

Brierton was happy the officers on the road would be fine to carry on without her hanging around, so she made her way back to her car and headed back to the station.

Nine

Garner was sitting at his desk in the team's office reading through the report Rachel Howton had sent him, it was not very long and as he reached the end of it Brierton walked back into the office.

Garner looked up at her and said, "There is not much to go on here but the body in the back of the van has been identified as David Warren. It looks like he was killed after being hit on the back of the head with the hammer that was found in the back of the van with his body. Howton's report also confirms that there is no blood in the van other than where the body was laying, so she is satisfied the lad was not killed in the van."

Brierton said, "That name rings bells." Parsons looked up from his desk and replied, "Yes, I just looked him up on the system and if it is the same David Warren I am looking at here, he has a string of arrests in the past for drug dealing. He seems to have some very strong links with a certain Mr Kurzwell."

Brierton then carried on by saying, "That fits in with what a witness heard from his house in College Street last night. He said he overheard someone shouting about someone called Mick not being very happy about something. It's possibly related to the white van parked in Cross Street which is opposite from where he lives."

Garner looked towards Brierton and said, "I bet he didn't see who was shouting, did he."

"No," replied Brierton, "he said that by the time he had got to his window all that he saw was a white van driving away. He said he didn't actually, see what had happened outside in the street."

Parsons replied to this with, "That's a shame, it sounds like he may have been able to tell us what took place in the street."

To which Brierton replied, "well, we may

have a bit of luck on that front yet. There is a camera mounted on a shop nearby that may have filmed what took place. One of the house-to-house officers is going to talk to the owner of the shop when it opens and see if they can provide us with the video files for yesterday."

Garner said, "So it looks like Kurzwell will be worth talking to about this at some point soon." To which Brierton replied, "Yeah, that'll please him. Especially after your chat with the Superintendent earlier."

Garner stood up from his desk and started to put his jacket on. As he did he said, "Alan, can you arrange a family liaison officer to meet us at David Warren's house." And then turning his attention towards Brierton he said, "We will head down and give them the bad news and see if we can get anything from them about David's movements for the last few days and see if that sheds any light on what has happened and why."

Brierton also got up from her desk and along with Garner headed for the office door and left. In the meantime, Parsons picked up his telephone and started to call the control room so a liaison officer could be assigned and sent down to the house where the Warrens lived.

Ten

As Garner and Brierton drove through the town towards David Warren's house Brierton said, "I have dealt with this family before, David and Joanna have both been mixed up with drugs for a few years. The parents have tried their best to guide them away from the local gangs but to no avail."

Garner said, "Right, do you want to take the lead on this then, seeing as you know them." Brierton replied, "Can do, I doubt it will be easy but they may remember me from the days I was in uniform and trying to help them out from time to time."

After a short time, Garner and Brierton arrived at the house where David Warren lived along with his family. As they approached the front door of the house it opened and a young girl stood in the doorway.

"Hello Joanna," said Brierton. To which the young girl replied, "Oh, it's you lot. I suppose you will be wanting to come in."

Brierton continued, "Yes, please. Are your parents in?"

This was met with silence and Joanna moved away from the door and headed into the house and then into the front room.

Brierton turned to Garner and said, "I guess she remembers me."

Brierton went into the room ahead of Garner and as she entered she saw David and Joanna's parents Paul and Andrea sitting, watching the television. As they entered the room Paul picked up the television remote and turned the television off and said, "crikey, you have not been here for a long time."

Brierton said, "No, I haven't. This is DCI Garner who is my boss. Is it alright if I sit down?"

Paul nodded and pointed towards a spare

chair against the wall and asked, "Sure sit down there."

Once Brierton had sat down she said, "I have some really bad news about David. I am sorry to tell you, but we found him dead this morning up on the Wilton Road Estate."

As Brierton finished speaking, Joanna started crying and ran out of the room, nearly knocking Garner off his feet.

Brierton carried on by saying, "We have a family liaison officer being sent down from the station who will stay with you while we try and find out what happened. I know this will be a horrible shock to you all, but I need to ask you some questions."

Paul asked, "What happened? Do you know who killed him?"

Brierton said, "That's what we are going to find out. We think he was attacked in the College Street area of Cleethorpes last night. Do you know if he was meeting anyone or heading somewhere in the evening?"

Neither Paul nor Andrea responded to this

but Joanna had now returned to the room and sat down opposite Brierton. Joanna said, "I think he was dealing there. I know I shouldn't tell you anything really but." As she started to carry on speaking, Paul chipped in and said, "what do you mean dealing? I thought you had both gotten out of that stupid business."

Joanna started to cry and said, "I'm sorry Dad but we tried to get out of it but the guy running the local drug scene would not let us stop. He said if we did not carry on he would have us killed."

As Joanna finished speaking, Garner moved further into the room and said, "Who made these threats towards you?"

Joanna started to cry even more and through her tears, she said, "I know I will get into more trouble with him if I tell you but I don't care anymore. It was Kurzwell, Mick Kurzwell."

Eleven

As Garner and Brierton were leaving the house another male officer was arriving at the front door. It was George Brown who was going to act as the family liaison officer on this case. Brown had been assigned to the case because like Brierton, he had a history of trying to help the family out in the past and it was thought this may help.

"Hello Becca, Sir," said Brown as he met Brierton and Garner coming out of the house.

Both Garner ad Brierton acknowledged the greeting from Brown with a, "Hello," and then Brierton said.

"Are you up to speed on what has happened to David?"

To which Brown replied.

"Yes. I have read the details of what has happened, but is there anything new from your visit to the family?"

Brierton said, "Yes, Joanna has told us that David and herself tried to get out of the drug dealing gang operating in the area but they had been threatened by Mick Kurzwell so they were forced to carry on dealing. I think she is so upset about David's death that she may be willing to spill the beans on Kurzwell and his operation."

Garner was now standing at the gate in front of the house. He had decided to leave Brierton and Brown to discuss things about the family as they both had knowledge of them and had both dealt with them in the past. Sometimes officers having a history with a family involved in a case as serious as this could be problematic, but he felt in this case it may help persuade Joanna to talk and the fact that the parents had been unaware of their kid's continued involvement with the drug scene may help put pressure on her to talk to the police.

Once Brierton and Brown had finished their conversation, Brown went into the house to speak to the family and explain what he was going to do to help them and Brierton walked to the gate to catch up with Garner.

As they walked back to Garner's car, Brierton was thinking about what David Warren's sister had said about Mick Kurzwell.

She said.

"With Kurzwell being mentioned a few times regarding this case, I suppose we will have to think about bringing him in to see what he has to say about all of this," she paused for a moment and then continued, "but what I don't understand is why would he kill David when David was doing what he was told. It would make more sense that Kurzwell was involved if David was refusing to work for him."

They had now reached the car and gone to opposite sides of it. Garner pressed the button on the key fob to open the doors and as he opened his door, he said.

"Your right, if it is Kurzwell behind this

then there must be something we don't know about. Let's head back to the station and see if Parsons has got anything from the CCTV system that will help us."

Just as Garner was about to drive away from the kerbside, he noticed Joanna leaving the house and getting on her moped that had been parked in the small front garden of the house. She started up the moped and put on her helmet. She then had a look around her and moved off, heading down the road in the same way Garner's car was facing so Garner decided to follow her and see where she was heading.

As Garner pulled away following Joanna on her moped, he said, "Let's see where she is off to."

Twelve

Joanna made her way through the streets of Cleethorpes from her home down to the seafront area followed by Garner and Brierton. Fortunately, she had stuck to the actual roads and not gone down any shortcuts because she would have easily lost her followers. Once at the seafront, she parked her moped to the side of the arcade near the Pier where Mick Kurzwell operated from and made her way through the arcade area to his office door at the rear.

Joanna shouted, "Why did you do it? Why did you kill David?" as she banged on his door repeatedly.

The door opened and standing in the doorway was Kurzwell himself.

"Stop shouting and come in," Kurzwell

said as he reached out and grabbed Joanna by the shoulder, pulling her into the office and closing the door behind her.

Joanna repeated in a loud voice, "why did you kill David? We carried on doing what you wanted, but you still killed him."

Kurzwell grabbed Joanna by the shoulders and said to her in a raised but not shouting voice, "I had nothing to do with David's death, so stop shouting at me or I will have something to do with you getting hurt."

Joanna started to cry again and said, "well, if it wasn't you then who was it?" to which Kurzwell replied.

"I don't know, I'm trying to find out myself, but no one seems to know anything about what happened. The best thing for you to do is carry on as usual and leave the rest to me. That way nothing else has to happen to anyone else. Especially you or the rest of your family. Now get out of here and get on with your deliveries."

Joanna froze momentarily at what Kurzwell had said to her. She remembered just how ruthless he can be and thought she might be better off leaving at this point.

So, she turned round towards the office door and walked back to it. She looked back towards Kurzwell and was going to make a threat towards him but thought better of it and left the office, letting the door close behind her. Joanna then ran through the arcade back to where she had left her moped. All she could think about was that once again she was living under the control of the man she had become to hate and fear the most.

Thirteen

As Joanna ran out of the arcade near the Pier, Garner and Brierton were still sitting in the car across the road watching and waiting to see what was going to happen next. Joanna got onto her moped and rode off.

Brierton said, "I would love to know what was said in there, do you think we should go and speak to Kurzwell?

Garner said, "I am not sure it is worth it. I am still not convinced he will know anything. If the Warren's where doing as he wanted, then I don't see what he has to gain from bringing all this attention onto himself and his activities. I don't think there's anything to gain here so let's head back to the station and see if Alan has come up with anything else from either the CCTV or ANPR systems."

Garner started the car and just as he was going to pull away and head back to the station his mobile started ringing. He took the phone out of his pocket and answered it saying "Garner." He listened for a few moments and then said, "OK Ma'am, I will see you then, bye." Once this call had ended, he put his phone back in his pocket and started to drive again back to the station.

Back in Kurzwell's office, Kurzwell was making a call on his mobile. Once the person he was calling had answered the call he said, "I think we need to keep a close watch on Joanna Warren. She has just been here shouting and balling about the death of her brother and it somehow being my fault. Get everyone to keep an eye on her and if she starts to become a problem then we may have to look at dealing with her.

Fourteen

As Garner arrived back at the team's office Parsons was sitting at his desk and said.

"Hi, I've been looking through the CCTV footage from the control room. I think you should see this video clip."

"Right, let's see," Garner replied and made his way around Parson's desk so he could sit beside him and see the screen on the desk.

Parsons took hold of his mouse and played a video clip. As he did this he said, "This clip shows the attack taking place. It doesn't show much detail but you can make out what happened."

Both concentrated on the screen and watched the clip. It showed what appeared to be a young male walking along the side street towards the high street with another person in dark clothing and wearing some sort of face covering following him. The video then showed the male being struck with what looked like a long thin object and then falling to the ground.

Almost immediately, a white van pulled up and within what seemed to be a few seconds pulled away again.

Parsons paused the clip and said, "So we know there are at least two people involved at this point." To which Garner replied, "Yes, and it looks as if both the attacker and victim left in the van, so this has got to be a planned attack."

"I think so as well," Parsons replied as he started playing the clip again. The footage showed the van pulling away from the kerbside and going out of view.

Once Parsons had stopped the video he said, "Although we cannot see which way the van went at the end of the road, we can be sure of its route after the attack because of the ANPR details we have.

Garner said, "Can you send a copy of this over to Howton? This may help her out with what the cause of death was."

"Will do," Parsons replied.

As Parsons was preparing to send the video off to Rachel Howton the office door opened and in walked Brierton and said.

"Hi, I've got us all coffee."

Garner replied, "Thanks, we have just been looking at the video footage from Cross Street. Might be worth you looking at it as it shows the attack of Dave Warren."

"OK," Brierton replied and made her way around Parson's desk, placed his coffee on his desk and sat down beside him as he played the video."

Brierton watched the video footage to the end and then said, "Hang on, the guy we spoke to who said he heard the shouting and saw the van driving off is wrong."

Garner got up from his desk, crossed the office and stood behind Parsons and Brierton and said, "What do you mean?"

"Well, he said that he heard shouting just before looking out of the window and seeing the van leaving. But, if you watch the video, Warren never turns around, which I would have expected him to do if someone behind him shouts at him. The video shows that he was walking along facing forward when he is struck," Brierton replied while looking at her notes, "it was a Dennis Owens, who claimed to have heard the shouting," she continued.

Garner asked Parsons to play the video again, which he did and then Garner said, "Bring him in and let's find out if he is mistaken or lying to us," to which Brierton replied with, "can we hang off doing that for a moment? Let me chase up the CCTV footage from the shop on the road. The camera on the side of the shop may show a slightly different view of the street so it may show more of what took place."

Garner said, "OK, see if you can get that footage and then we will decide what to do next in the morning. I'm heading out now as I have a meeting with Superintendent Jones, so I'll see you two in the morning."

Fifteen

Sitting in a meeting room on the top floor of the police station were Superintendent Jones and two officers from the National Crime Agency. They had been talking for an hour or so and were finishing off the discussion as Garner entered the room.

Jones said, "come on in Robert, we are just finishing off here so I will discuss things with you."

As Jones finished speaking, the two NCA officers got up from their chairs. Both the officers lent over the table and shook hands with Superintendent Jones. One of the officers said, "Thank you for your time, Ma'am, we will keep in touch with you with anything new we come up with if you can do the same for us."

Jones said, "Yes, that's fine."

At this, the two visitors headed for the office door, as they left the room the second officer looked at Garner and said, "Evening DCI Garner, sorry we cannot stay for a full introduction, but I expect we will see each other again soon," and closed the door behind him.

Once Garner and Superintendent Jones were alone in the room, Jones said, "come and sit down and I'll explain what is going on here."

Garner made his way across the room and sat down at the table. He was not aware of what was going to be said, as he had thought that this meeting was to be him updating Superintendent Jones on the current case. There had been a lot of local media coverage and the Superintendent liked to be up to date with the facts of cases that she knew she would be contacted about by the press. But the presence of the two NCA officers in the room meant something else was going to be discussed.

Once both Garner and Jones were sitting Jones said.

"Those two officers have been updating

me about an ongoing operation taking place in the area. It appears that with all the improvements being made to security on the south coast, a lot more drugs are being imported via the Port in Immingham. Now, you are being briefed about this because of your dealings with the local dealer Kurzwell. He is helping the NCA with information about what is going on."

Garner said, "I see, you are aware that his name has come up in our enquiries into the death of the Warren lad in Cleethorpes last night?"

Jones said, "Yes, that's what prompted the NCA visit. When his name was put on the system as having made threats towards the Warren kids a Red Flag popped up on the system. The next thing I know is that I get told the NCA wanted to speak to me and, here we are."

"Well, we couldn't work out why Kurzwell would want to have David Warren killed and with what you are telling me, it is unlikely he would be wanting to draw attention to himself at this point if he is helping the NCA," Garner said.

Jones replied, "That would make sense. Can you try and avoid all contact with him if at all possible for the next couple of days? Obviously, if he is involved then bring him in but maybe try and do it discreetly."

Garner said, "Will do, I guess I need to keep the team in the dark about this."

To which Superintendent Jones replied, "Yes, I'm afraid so. Once the operation at the port is complete, which I understand will be within the next couple of days, you can tell them everything. But for now, it's on a need-to-know level. One good thing is that there's a good chance Kurzwell will be out of our hair after this one as I understand he is going into witness protection and being moved out of the area."

Jones then picked up her large leather folder and said "That's it for the night, so I'll see you tomorrow Robert," and headed out of the room.

Garner sat for a few moments thinking about the fact that he would have to keep what was going on a secret from his team. This was not something he would enjoy as they were a new team and he knew there had to be trust between them to work well together. As he got up from his chair to head out of the room and head home, he thought to himself that it would be alright as hopefully there would not be any need to bring Kurzwell in, in the future.

Sixteen

Parsons, Garner and Brierton were all in early today as they had all received a message in the early hours saying that the CCTV footage from the shop across the road from where the Cross Street attack had taken place had been sent through.

The footage had taken a while to arrive as it was the owner's son that was the only person who knew how to get the footage off the system and email it to the police. Unfortunately, he had been working out of town for a couple of days so was unable to help until his return to the area.

Parsons sat down at his desk and started looking through the clips so he could view the ones recorded around the same time as the attack and abduction of David Warren. It took a bit of time as the shop owner's son had sent through videos covering the whole day in question.

Once Parsons had found the file covering the time of the attack, he opened it and started watching. For the most part, it showed the same events as the footage sent through from the police control room as the camera covered the same area of the street but from a different angle.

The main difference with this new footage is that it showed what took place on the other side of the van that had been out of view from the original police footage. This view showed that the attacker had hit David Warren from behind and when the van pulled up the attacker opened the side door and lifted David into the van and closed the door again. Then before the van pulled away, the attacker ran down a passage between some buildings and into the darkness.

Parsons called Garner and Brierton over to his desk and showed them the new footage.

Garner watched the video and said, "this throws a completely different light on what happened in Cross Street. Allan, can you get the footage from the cameras at the other end of the passage and see if the attacker appears again? Then see if you can work out where they go next."

Parsons said, "that'll take some time so I will get straight onto it now."

Garner said, "right, I'll go and get the coffees," to which Brierton replied, "better make Allan's a large one."

Garner then left the office and Brierton sat down at her desk and started reviewing all the statements and notes she had about the case.

After about an hour Parson's looked up from his desk and once again called Garner and Brierton over to his desk. He had lined up some of the many video clips he had gathered and started to play them on his computer screen.

As the videos started to play, he said, "here we see the actual attack. But rather than the attacker getting into the van as we had first thought, the attacker runs off down the passage before the van pulls away. Now, if we look at the video clip taken at the other end of the passage shortly after the attack, we see a person coming out of the passage. The person is the same height and build but is wearing a light-coloured top and no face covering."

Brierton said, "So, either this is not the attacker but a witness that may have seen or heard the attack take place or it's the attacker and they took their top and face covering off while coming through the passage."

Garner then said, "right, can you carry on looking through the footage? to see if you can work out where that person heads to and we will go and organise a more thorough search of the passageway to see if we can locate that jacket and face covering. That will help us work out if it is a suspect or a witness."

Parsons said, "OK, I will call you if I find anything new."

Garner and Brierton then left the office and made their way to the station's control room where they spoke to the duty sergeant and arranged for as many officers as possible to make their way to Cross Street where they could be organised into a search party to try and locate the jacket and face covering worn by the attacker that may have been dumped somewhere along the passageway.

Seventeen

College and Cross Streets were both now full of police cars and vans. Uniformed officers were standing around in various-sized groups where the streets met and were waiting to be organised into search parties and given the order to go ahead with the search of the area.

Another marked police car pulled up at the junction of the two streets and a uniformed sergeant got out of the passenger's side. He made his way to the entrance of the passageway where he stopped and turned round towards the other officers.

He bellowed in a deep gruff voice, "Gather round."

The sound of his voice made all the other officers stop talking and quickly make their way from where they were standing and over to his location where they gathered in front of him.

The sergeant then continued by pointing towards four officers standing in front of him and saying, "right, you four start by making your way down the passage. It's your lucky day, it's bin day and there are lots of bins out but you get to just look around them, so off you go and remember, we are looking for a dark jacket."

As the first four officers formed a line across the entrance to the passage and started to make their way down it the sergeant turned his attention to the rest of the officers standing in front of him and said.

"I need you, you and you," pointing to three other officers, "go along the front of the houses in College Street and tell anyone who is in, that other officers will be entering their backyards either through or over their back gates or walls. There is no point people calling the station about being worried about someone appearing in their back garden."

As he finished speaking the three officers hurried away back along Cross Street and back into College Street to carry out the Sergeant's order. As they did so the Sergeant once again turned his attention to the remaining officers standing in front of him.

"OK, form two lines, one on either side of the passage and follow me. You're the lucky ones getting to search the bins and gardens."

As the officers got themselves into lines the Sergeant started to walk down the centre of the passageway. Whenever he arrived at a bin or a rear gate to a property he stopped, turned around and pointed the officer at the front of the line on the side of the passage and said, "OK, you check that out." And as an officer carried out this order he turned and continued down the passage, followed by his two lines of officers.

Eventually, the Sergeant ran out of officers to search bins or enter the rear yards. So, he had to wait for officers to finish carrying out their current search task and then rejoin him further along the passage. This was going to slow down progress but that's the way it had to be.

As the search continued, Garner and Brierton arrived at Cross Street. As they approached the passage they could see the searching officers were busy and that the Sergeant in charge of them was controlling the search from further down the passage. Garner waved towards the Sergeant who acknowledged his presence by waving back.

Garner said, "let's head back to the car and let these guys get on with the search. We will probably just get in the way if we stay out here."

Eighteen

After about two hours of searching a loud shout came from an officer standing in a gateway a little way back along the passage from where the sergeant was now standing, sending other officers into back gardens, or pointing to the next bin that needed checking.

"Sergeant, I have something here."

The Sergeant shouted back, "OK, hang on and I'll be right there." Then, turning to the next officer to be assigned a task, he said, "you take over what I am doing and assign the next officer to either a bin or yard." And he then made his way back to where the officer who had called him was standing.

"What you got?" The sergeant asked the officer.

To which the officer replied, "In here," and made his way back through the rear gate of a house that backed onto the passageway. The officer then raised the lid of another bin in the rear yard so that the Sergeant could look in and see a dark jacket under a bag of rubbish that had been either dropped in afterwards or moved in an attempt to hide the jacket.

The sergeant said, "right, you wait here, and I'll get the DCI and DS down here."

The sergeant grabbed his radio and pressed the call button. Once he had contacted the control room back in the station he said, "can you let DCI Garner know we have found something about halfway down the passageway and ask him to join us."

"OK, will do." Came the reply from the control room.

The sergeant and the officer who had found the jacket waited by the bin for the arrival of Garner and Brierton who had been contacted by the control room and were making their way down.

As they joined the two officers at the bin,

Garner said, "hi, the station told us you have made a find, but did not give any details."

The uniformed officer said, "yes sir, I found what looks like the jacket you're looking for in this bin."

Brierton looked into the bin and said, "looks like it might be the one, can you get it out please."

The uniformed officer leaned towards the bin and reached in. He grabbed the jacket and gently raised it out so everyone standing around the bin could see it. Once he had lifted it clear of the bin opening, he held it up so Brierton could get a good look at it. Brierton compared the jacket to the one being worn by the attacker in an image she had on her mobile for a few moments and then said.

"Yes, it looks like the jacket we are looking for and that looks like a woolly hat in the pocket. I bet that's what the attacker used as a face covering during the attack. Can we get it bagged so we can take it back to the station for a proper check?"

The Sergeant then held up an evidence

bag and said, "drop it in here."

The officer placed the jacket into a large evidence bag that the Sergeant was holding open and then the Sergeant sealed the bag up and passed it to Brierton.

Brierton said, "thanks, can you carry on with the search? I don't think there will be anything else but you never know."

"Will do," said the Sergeant, "it'll keep this lot out of bother for a while if I keep them here."

Garner said, "thanks for that. We will head back to the station with this jacket. Call us if you find anything else." Then, turning to Brierton, he said, "let's head back and get the jacket to Rachel Howton."

As they started to make their way back to Garner's car, his mobile started to ring. They both stopped walking and Garner pulled out his phone. He said, "it's Allan, hopefully, he has got something for us from the CCTV cameras."

"Hi Allan," Garner said after answering the call on his mobile phone.

The voice at the other end of the call said, "hi, I have some interesting information for you. Are you with Becca?"

Garner replied, "yes, she's here, I'll put you on speaker."

Nineteen

Once both Garner and Brierton could listen in on the call Garner said, "OK Allan, go ahead."

Allen then said, "I have just emailed you both two extracts from the shop CCTV we got. I carried on looking into where the person coming out of the passageway went after they emerged at the other end and worked out that they had gone back along College Street towards where the attack took place. I then looked at the clips from the shop and saw the person going back into one of the houses near the attack location."

Garner said, "that's great," and turning to Brierton he said, "can you get that video up on your phone?"

Brierton replied, "yes, one moment."

"OK, carry on Allan," Garner said into his phone.

Parsons then went on to say, "I cannot work out which house number they go into which is why I thought I would send it through to you guys so you can have a look and work out which house it is."

Garner said, "we will have a look and see if we can work it out. What does the second clip you sent through show us?"

Parsons said, "well, that is the really interesting thing. Because of what the first clip showed, I thought I would look back in the day to see if I could work out the house number but even in the daylight I was unable to see that much detail but I did see a person leaving the house wearing what looked like the jacket you were looking for in the passageway."

Garner said, "OK, Becca is looking at the second video clip now."

As Brierton was watching the second video she muttered, "that's interesting," looked up from her phone and said, "that looks like David Owens leaving the house in the earlier clip and coming back in the later one. So, if it is him there is no way he was a witness as he claimed but more likely that he was the actual attacker."

Twenty

Two uniformed officers had now made their way around to the back of the Owens's house and were standing by the rear garden gate. One of them said, "We are in position at the rear of the house." Into his radio which signalled to the officers standing with Garner and Brierton at the front of the house to knock on the door.

Brierton knocked on the front door and after a short while, the door of the house opened and standing in the doorway was Dennis Owens.

Brierton said, "Hello Mr Owens, we need to come in and talk to you about the attack that took place over the road," to which Owens said, "no thanks," and started to shut the door. As he tried to close the door, one of the uniformed officers moved forward past Brierton and pushed the door open again and forcing his way into the house.

Owens ran through the house followed by the uniformed officer who had forced the door back open and Brierton towards the back door. As he approached the rear door of the house he could see the two officers that had made their way into the rear garden and were now standing at the rear door and prepared to stop anyone leaving that way.

Within seconds of all this taking place, the uniformed officer had grabbed Owens and as he was moving his arms behind him to enable him to be handcuffed, Brierton told him his rights.

Brierton said, "Dennis Owens, I am arresting you on suspicion of the murder of David Warren."

As she said this, Owens pulled away from the officer behind him and barged past Brierton. As he made his way back through the house he moved close to where Garner was standing and as he tried to push past, Garner grabbed Owen's arm and stuck his foot in front of him, causing Owens to fall to the floor but in a controlled manner as Garner still had hold of his arm.

Brierton was now standing next to Garner and said, "nice move sir, good to see you still have it."

Garner looked towards Brierton and said, "saves having to chase anyone," and turning to a couple of officers now standing in the doorway of the house, he said, "pick him up and take him to the station. We will follow and talk to him when we get there."

As the officers picked Owens up, he said, "you've got nothing on me, you'll not be pinning this one on me."

Garner replied to this by saying, "I think you'll find we have plenty on you and the fact you have played up here suggests you know you're in trouble."

Twenty-One

Once Owens had been taken into the front room of the house and sat down in a chair, Garner took his mobile out of his pocket and called back to the station.

He said, "Hi, DCI Garner here, I am in College street and have just made an arrest. Can you send a van to pick him up and transport him back to the station," then paused to allow for a response, then said, "thanks, bye," and ended the call.

Garner, Brierton and the officers in the house started to look around for anything that may help them prove Dennis Owens was responsible for the attack and killing of David Warren. As they did Brierton called out to Garner.

She said, "sir, look at this photo here in the front room."

Garner made his way into the small front room and joined Brierton who was holding a picture frame containing a photograph of two adult men and a young girl.

Brierton said, "these two look very alike, I wonder if they are twins."

Garner took the photo frame from Brierton and studied it closely. He said, "they do, have a look around and see if there is anything here that will confirm Owens has a brother and if either of them has a daughter."

Everyone in the house continued to search and after about twenty minutes one of the uniformed officers searching upstairs called down to Garner and Brierton, "Sir, Sergeant Brierton, can you both come up here please?"

Brierton called back, "OK, what have you found?"

The officer said, "I heard you say about Owen's maybe having a brother and thought you may find these papers interesting."

The officer handed Garner some pieces of

paper which he started to study.

Garner then said, "this is very useful, these papers show that Dennis Owen has a twin brother and that the brother had a daughter. Look, this is a death certificate showing that the girl had died as a result of a car accident."

Garner handed Brierton the death certificate and said, "call the station and get an alert out for the brother and see if they can send you the details of the case. In the meantime, let's head back to the station."

Twenty-Two

Mick Kurzwell and the two NCA officers who had been in the meeting with Superintendent Jones earlier were sitting in the living room of a house in Immingham near the entrance of the port area. They had been discussing how the drug gang based in London were planning to bring a large shipment of drugs into the country via the port.

Kurzwell was going to meet up with the lorry containing the drugs later and then travel to London with the driver to meet up with the gang.

"Right, it's time you headed out," one of the officers said to Kurzwell, "remember we will be watching from here and there are various teams that are going to follow you down to London and the final meeting."

Kurzwell said, "OK, I will see you later with a bit of luck."

Kurzwell then stood up and grabbed his jacket from the arm of the seat he had been sitting in and headed out of the room towards the back door of the house. The two NCA officers then headed up the stairs and into a bedroom which had been equipped with a video camera. One of the officers moved a net curtain covering the window a small amount so he could see out of the window. The officer could see the entrance of the port in the distance and Kurzwell, who was now standing on the corner of the road where it met the main road that led from the port to the A180 which is the route out of the area and onwards to London.

Inside the port, there was a lot of activity with the movement of containers that had arrived from around the world. The containers had arrived on ships and once unloaded moved to storage locations around the port. One of these containers had now been loaded onto a lorry that was heading out of the port through the main exit. Once the port security officer, located at the port exit had checked the driver's paperwork, he waved the lorry through the gates. The lorry made its way out of the port and onto the road that led away from the port.

A few minutes after the lorry left the port it pulled up at the road junction where Kurzwell was standing. Kurzwell opened the passenger door of the lorry and got in, closing the door behind him.

Kurzwell said, "right, let's get going, we have a long journey ahead of us." To which the driver replied with just a nod of his head and then started to move the lorry on its way. After a few hundred yards, a car pulled out of another side road and started to follow the lorry.

Back in the house, the two NCA officers started to pack up the video recorder as soon as the lorry containing Kurzwell and the drugs moved out of sight.

One of the officers said, "that's them on their way. Let's get this stuff packed up and head off. We need to be available to take over from the team following at the moment so the driver does not get suspicious of the same car following them, all the way to London."

The two officers then made their way out of the house and to their car which was parked outside. They placed their recording equipment into the boot of the car and then headed off to catch up with the lorry and the car that was currently following it.

Twenty-Three

Dennis Owens had now been taken from his cell and was sitting in an interview room with his solicitor within the police station waiting to be interviewed in connection with the abduction and murder of David Warren. His solicitor had already advised Owens to say nothing as they needed to know what evidence the police had before giving anything away from their side.

They had been waiting in the room for about an hour when the door opened and in walked Garner and Brierton.

Brierton immediately pressed the record button on the recording system on the table and said, "interview with Dennis Owens, present are DS Brierton, DCI Garner and Mr Owens solicitor."

Garner said, "Apologies for keeping you waiting but the search carried out in your house took longer than expected and we have also now started looking for your brother. We would like to speak to him about the killing of David Warren as well as we believe he was involved. Do you know where he is?"

Owens looked at his solicitor who just shook his head, indicating to Owens that he should not tell the police anything at this point. Even if it does not relate to himself directly.

Owens looked back towards Garner and said, "No comment."

Garner replied, "OK, here is what we have" and opened a folder of paperwork on the table in front of him.

He continued, "we have CCTV showing you leaving your house before the attack, abduction and murder of David Warren."

At this point, Brierton switched on the laptop she had brought with her to the interview room, started to play the CCTV footage showing Owens leaving his house, and turned the laptop around, so Owens and his solicitor could view the footage.

Brierton said, "We have the jacket you were wearing in this video and it is being tested for your DNA and David Warren's blood as we speak and we are confident there will be matches for both. How confident are you that there will not be matches?"

Once again Owens looked at his solicitor, who once again shook his head.

Owens said, "No comment."

Brierton then started to play the CCTV footage that showed the actual attack on David Warren and said, "here you can see David being attacked and thrown into the van and driven off. Do you have anything to say about what is going on in this video?"

Owens gave the same, "no comment" answer to this question that he had been advised to give in response to anything asked by the police.

Garner intervened in Brierton's questioning and said, "OK, since, we are not going to get anything from Mr Owens, we will leave this for now and wait for the DNA results from the jacket."

Brierton said, "interview suspended."

Garner and Brierton gathered their paperwork, stood up and walked towards the door. Garner turned back towards Dennis Owens and said.

"Once we have got the results from the DNA tests we will continue with this interview and I expect the questions will be a lot tougher then."

Brierton had now opened the door of the interview room and both she and Garner left the room.

Twenty-Four

Garner and Brierton had not got far along the corridor when the door of the interview room opened and George Owen's legal adviser appeared in the doorway and called out.

"Can you come back in please, my client would like to make a statement."

Both Garner and Brierton turned back towards the interview room door and made their way back into the room, closing the door behind them.

Once Garner, Brierton and the solicitor had sat back down, Brierton went through the procedure to restart the recording device and then Garner said, "please go ahead."

Owens then started to speak, I and the

other residents of the street where we live had to endure years of these scum drug dealers dealing their drugs in the street. They have made our lives a misery and you have never bothered to do anything about it. I was on my way out the other night when I spotted the Warren lad dealing on the corner of the street, I lost my temper and hit him. I didn't mean to kill him."

Brierton said, "I don't think that is anywhere near the truth, is it? We know you lied about hearing shouting outside your house and the fact that the van which we believe was being driven by your brother was stolen and arrived at the same time as the attack shows us this was all planned."

Garner then said, "again, we will leave this for now and wait for the test results on the jacket we found and take things from there. If you have any idea of your brother's whereabouts then it will be best to tell us now."

Owens returned to his advised position and said, "no comment."

Garner turned to Brierton and said, "let's

leave this for now and let Mr Owens talk with his solicitor for a bit longer. You never know, he may come up with a better explanation for why he killed David Warren."

Brierton then said, "interview concluded," and pressed the stop button on the recording system.

Once outside the interview room, Garner said to Brierton, "can you go along to the control room and see if there is any progress on locating the Owen brother? I think the quicker we find him the quicker we will find out what this is all about."

Brierton replied, "OK, will do. What about the statement Dennis Owen's just made? It was a confession wasn't it?"

Garner started to walk back towards the team's office and as he did, he said, "I think we can take it as that, although, the evidence we have means we don't need it anyway but I have a feeling it is not as simple as what he says it is. If there is no progress on locating the brother, head off for the night and we will see where we are in the morning."

Twenty-Five

Weaving her way in and out of traffic and riding down side passages throughout the town, Joanna was making her way to the evening customers who had called what had become known as the local Drugaroo hotline and placed their orders.

Using a moped had become the easiest and quickest way to make deliveries these days. Demand for small amounts of drugs had become the norm and like the general change in trends for purchasing, people had changed to having their fixes delivered and wanted it straight away.

Joanna had already made a few deliveries and was on her way towards her next delivery point when she became aware that another moped rider might be following her, and going by the sound coming from behind her, she knew the person following her was on a much more powerful bike, which meant she would probably not be able to outrun them.

However, she knew she could use her knowledge of the side roads and alleys in the area to try and shake off the other rider. She turned off the road she was on and into an alley that had a few narrow parts and would bring her out further up the road, but hoped the width of the alley would force anyone following her to slow down and give her time to disappear into another alley further up the road.

The main worry for Joanna at this time was that it was a police officer following her on the other bike and that they were in contact with other officers in the area which meant she had to be extra vigilant from now on. She knew that if it was the police she could be stopped at any moment and she still had pockets, full of various drugs she was dropping off, and, if searched it would be obvious she was dealing so would end up being arrested and taken to the police station and although this would be a nuisance it would bring more hassle from her boss for losing his drugs and the money she was to collect when making the deliveries.

Joanna was now nearing her next drop and as she rode slowly to the prearranged drop-off point which was a lay-by near some flats she saw a woman standing at the roadside waiting for her. As Joanna pulled up near the woman she realised it was the usual person who ordered at this location, so just had to take the money from her and hand over the ordered drugs without any meaningful chatter. Once the deal had been made the customer walked away and Joanna got ready to head off to the next drop-off point.

She looked around to see if there was any traffic coming along the road but could not see any so pulled away from the lay-by, crossed over the road and headed back the way she had come from. As she made her way along the road Joanna became aware that a car was catching up with her at speed. She looked in her mirror and could see the car was driving along behind her with only its side lights on. Within a few seconds of looking back at the car, it sped up and was now right behind Joanna and getting closer. All of a sudden, Joanna felt the bike she was riding jolt forward and realised she had been hit from behind but before she could do anything she had run into the back of a parked car and been thrown off her bike and into the road. As she landed on the road surface the car that had been following her ran straight over her, and then drove off at speed.

As the car drove off, a couple of people who saw what had happened ran into the road where Joanna's lifeless body was laying.

Twenty-Six

The lorry with Kurzwell in the passenger seat had driven through the night on its way down to London with just a couple of stops for the calls of nature and was now pulling into an industrial estate on the outskirts of the city. As it approached a warehouse within the estate Kurzwell made a call on his mobile telephone.

He said, "we are approaching now," and after a short pause he ended the call.

As he replaced his mobile into his jacket pocket the roller door of the warehouse started to raise and once the door was fully opened, the lorry drove into the warehouse and stopped. As Kurzwell and the driver got out of the lorry's cab, two men moved straight in and started removing a panel from the side of the lorry's cargo area. Once the panel had been removed, one of the men took out a small package and cut it open. A few seconds later he looked at Kurzwell and the driver and said, "everything looks good here."

Kurzwell said to the driver, "right, that's our job done. So, we had better make ourselves scarce and let these guys do their stuff."

The driver of the lorry then got back into the lorry's cab and grabbed two holdalls from behind the driver's seat. He then passed one of the holdalls to Kurzwell and the two of them left the warehouse via a rear door and got into a car waiting to take them away from the area.

Twenty-Seven

Garner, Brierton and Parsons had all received messages about the death of Joanna Warren in the early hours of the morning and had all made their way into the team's office. Superintendent Jones had called Garner and told him to take on the case because it involved the family of their current murder case and it was thought there is probably a link. Uniformed officers were already with Joanna's family, so there was no need for anyone from the team to visit them at this time.

Garner and Brierton were sitting at Garner's desk discussing the report that had been sent through about Joanna's killing when Parsons called over to them.

He said, "I have the details regarding the death of the Owens child. The case didn't result in any prosecutions as the inquest recorded it as an accident."

Garner said, "who was involved?"

Parsons looked further down the report and said, "the child who died was George Owen's daughter. The report then shows who was driving the car that killed her. It was Paul Warren."

A stunned silence fell in the room for a moment.

Brierton then broke the silence by saying, "that's David and Joanna Warren's father."

Garner said, "right, we need to locate the brother as I would bet my life he knows something about all of this and I wouldn't be surprised if he was responsible for Joanna's death last night," looking towards Brierton, he continued, "can you get on to the control room and see if we cannot get the search for him widened to cover the whole of the county rather than just the local area."

As Garner finished speaking, the office door opened and Superintendent Jones walked in and said, "Hello everyone, I'm sorry to disturb you as I know you're all very busy, " and looking at Garner, continued, "can I have a quick word with you, Robert."

Garner replied, "Yes, ma'am," and walked back out of the office with the Superintendent.

Twenty-Eight

Garner and Superintendent Jones were now in one of the small offices along the corridor from the team's own office.

As Jones closed the door behind them she said, "I want to give you an update on what we talked about the other evening regarding the NCA and Mick Kurzwell."

Garner replied, "right, are things moving forward on that?"

"Yes." Replied Jones, "the truck carrying the drugs was allowed to get through customs in Immingham and then made its way to London. Picking up Kurzwell just along the road from the docks. Once the truck arrived in London the NCA and armed officers cornered the gang members on an industrial estate and arrested them all."

Garner said, "what about Kurzwell, did he play along with everything?"

Jones replied, "yes, all the gang members have been taken to different locations so it would not look odd if he was taken away on his own and the rest together. I have spoken to the NCA officer in charge and he tells me they are satisfied that with the information Kurzwell has provided them with and the drugs now in their possession, they can arrest the remaining gang members and close down the import operation once and for all."

She then opened the office door and started to leave the room. As she did, she looked back and said, "How is the current case going?"

Garner replied, "we are confident that the Owen brothers are responsible for both deaths. Dennis, who we have in custody has confessed to his involvement in David Warren's murder and once we locate his brother George we are confident we will be able to prove his involvement with David's death and hopefully Joanna's as well."

Jones then left the room followed by

Garner.

As Garner came out of the room, Brierton was coming along and called out, "sir."

Garner stopped and turned towards Brierton and said, "what's up?

Brierton replied, "we have found George Owens. He was found sleeping in his car just in a layby just outside town. He has been arrested and is being brought in right now. I have also called Rachel Howton as the officers reported that the car he was in had damage to the front of it and a large dent on the bonnet and what looked like blood.

Twenty-Nine

Interviewing George Owens had been put off until the morning after his arrest, due to him being drunk when he was found. He had been brought into the station, checked over by the station's duty doctor and then locked up in a cell for the night so he could sober up.

The team had come into the office early to see if they could proceed with interviewing Owens first thing and were now all sitting in the office drinking tea and coffee when a uniformed officer came into the office to speak to them.

The officer said, "that's George Owens awake and in interview room one with a solicitor sir."

To which Garner replied, "thanks, we will give them a few minutes to talk and then come down and interview him."

As Garner finished his cup of tea, which was the real reason for wanting a small delay in going down to the interview room, he said, "Allan, can you call Rachel Howton and see if she has anything from the car and come down to the interview room with anything she gives you."

Parsons nodded and said, "will do," then reached for his telephone and started to dial the number for Howton's office.

Both Garner and Brierton then got up from their desks and headed out of the office to go down and interview George Owens about his involvement in the killings of David and Joanna Warren.

As they headed along the corridor from their office Garner and Brierton were met by Superintendent Jones coming the other way. She said, "I thought I would let you know that Mr and Mrs Warren are in the station. It looks like one of the officers at their house let it slip that the Owen brothers are being held concerning their kid's deaths and they want to know what is going on."

Garner replied, "OK, we will update them as soon as we can but with Mr Warren's link to the death of George Owen's daughter it will be better if we could get them to go home as any update is likely to kick things off with them."

Jones said, "right, I'll see if I can get them to leave and go back home."

Once the discussion with Jones had finished, Garner and Brierton continued to make their way to the interview room where George Owens and his solicitor were waiting. They entered the room and sat down at the table in the middle of the room.

Thirty

Brierton arranged her paperwork in front of her and proceeded to start the recording equipment and said, "this recording is of an interview with Mr George Owens, present in the room, is me, DS Brierton, DCI Garner, Mr George Owens and his legal representative."

Garner then started the interview with, "Morning Mr Owens, how are you feeling now?"

Owens replied, "no comment."

Garner then said, "we have video footage of the attack and abduction of David Warren involving the use of a small white van. We believe it was you driving the van and then making your way to the Wilton Road estate and leaving the van there. What do you say to this allegation?"

Owens replied, "no comment."

Garner said, "we believe the damage to your car was caused by you driving into the moped Joanna Warren was riding and killing her. Do you have anything to say about that?"

Owens again replied with, "no comment."

Brierton said, "it looks like you have been briefed to say nothing during this interview which is your right but as I am sure you know, we have your brother in custody and has confessed to the killing of David Warren. The only thing keeping us from charging you both with his killing now is that we are waiting for the details of the DNA found in the van."

Garner continued, "we are happy that the CCTV footage and your brother's confession are all we need to charge him with the killing. Once we have the DNA results from the van we believe you will be charged as well. Do you have anything to say about that?"

Once again Owens replied with a simple, "no comment."

As Garner was about to start talking again the door of the room opened and Parsons walked in.

Brierton looked around and saw who it was and said, "for the recording, Allan Parsons has entered the room."

Parsons made his way to the table where everyone was sitting and placed a piece of paper on the table in front of Garner and said, "this is the information from the examination of the car Mr Owens was found sleeping in last night." He then left the room again.

While Garner read the paper, Brierton said, "for the recording, Allan Parsons has now left the room again."

Garner then passed the piece of paper to Brierton to read and then a moment later said, "the examination of the bonnet area of your car has shown that what looked like blood on it is the same blood type as Joanna Warren. It also shows that paint matching the colour of her moped has been found on the front of your car within the dent. Do you have a comment to make on this?"

Owens looked round at his solicitor, who looked at Owens and then said, "I think I need some time with my client to discuss this."

Thirty-One

Garner and his team had now gathered all the evidence relating to the deaths of David and Joanna Warren and passed it on to the crown prosecution service, who had come back with how the Owen brothers should be charged. Dennis Owens was to be charged with the murder of David Warren and George Owens could be charged with the murder of Joanna Warren and for the abduction and manslaughter of David Warren and both were now being held in custody and awaiting trial.

Meanwhile:-

Sitting in the living room of a safe house in London were Mick Kurzwell and two National Crime agency officers. These officers had been assigned to protect Kurzwell while efforts were made to round up the remaining members of a large crime family based in London. Kurzwell had been a junior member of the family many years ago and knew a lot about the remaining members who the NCA were trying to apprehend and prosecute.

Kurzwell had decided to turn informer a few months prior because he had become concerned for his safety due to the knowledge he was planning to hand over to the authorities.

As the three men waited in the London safe house the front doorbell rang. One of the officers got up and made their way to the door and opened it.

Standing in the doorway were two more NCA officers who had come to take Kurzwell to a local NCA office to be interviewed further.

The officer who had opened the door called back to where the other officer and Kurzwell were sitting.

"Come on then, let's go." He called and Kurzwell and the other officer reacted to the call by getting up from their seats and making their way to the door.

As they left the house all the officers continually looked around them as there was a real threat to Kurzwell's safety and they were fully aware that people were on the lookout for any chance to kill him to stop him talking. Once Kurzwell and the two officers who had come to pick him up were in the car, that would take him away the car pulled off, followed by a second car with more officers inside following closely.

The two officers that had been in the house with Kurzwell then went back inside to gather all their and Kurzwell's belongings together ready to move to the next safe house as it had been decided to move Kurzwell regularly to protect him.

Once the car containing Kurzwell had arrived at the NCA offices, he was led inside and into a room where he was told he would have to wait until the interview team arrived. After about ten minutes of waiting, Kurzwell's attention was drawn towards the door of the room that had now opened. Two people entered the room. The first person was unknown to him, but the second one who entered the room was someone whom he had not only had dealings with recently but had crossed paths with in the past when he worked for the London crime family.

It was DCI Garner, who had been called down to London to help with the operation that was being planned to round up the remaining members of the crime family he and the team he worked with before had targeted.

About the Author

John Messingham was born in Hampton, Middlesex, England. After finishing school, he joined the British Army and served as an Infantryman and later trained as a radio operator within the battalion mortar platoon. After his time in the army, he trained as a computer programmer and started a long career in IT. The fiction he writes sometimes draws on both his military and IT backgrounds.

For more information about John and his writing, please visit:

https://johnmessingham.co.uk

By John Messingham

DCI Garner and DS Brierton Novelettes

Series One

The Pier

The Body in the Van

Murder in the Park

Short Stories

The Water Thieves

Reece Leach Short Stories One

The Watchers

Printed in Great Britain
by Amazon